Beneath the Layers of Me

An Anthology Curated by

Jumana Presswala

Inkfeathers Publishing
www.inkfeathers.com

Beneath the Layers of Me
Edited & Compiled by Jumana Presswala
Print Edition

First Published in India in 2022
Inkfeathers Publishing
New Delhi 110095

ISBN 9789390882236

www.inkfeathers.com

Featuring the writings of

Teresa Terly, Sarah Siamwala, Lakshmi Yazhini, Anakha Raj

Srushti Chavan, Fatema Setranjiwala, Ben Holdeman

Michael Girasoli, Spruha Rajwadkar, Insiya Arsiwala

Anju Elizabeth Kurien, Suhani Shah, Giuseppe Li Santi

Rana Dhvani, Rajshree Nipane, Erin Staley, Shabnam Islam

Kriti Bhatia, Sakina Mahableshwarwala, Klaudine Palma

Asad Umar, Ayesha Anam Althaf, Krushita Sampath

Fatima Mackizadeh, Arwa Ratlamwala, Khushi Kalra

Misbah Iram, Komal Joshi, Rishika Priyadarsi, Ananya Singh

Riya Dugar, Siddhi Patil, Aanika Gajendragad, Remnik Gill

Harshit Dudhani, Arfa Fathima A

Disclaimer

The anthology 'Beneath the Layers of Me' is a collection of 5 short stories and 37 poems written by 35 authors who belong to different parts of the world.

Unless otherwise indicated, all the names, characters, objects, businesses, places, events, incidents—whether physical/non-physical, real/unreal, tangible/ intangible in whatsoever description used in this book are either the product of the author's imagination or used in a fictitious manner. Any resemblance to actual persons, objects, entities, living or dead, or actual events is purely coincidental.

The poems & stories published in this book are solely owned by their respective authors and are in no way intended to hurt anyone's religious, political, spiritual, brand, personal or fanatic beliefs and/or faith, whatsoever. In case, any sort of plagiarism is detected in the contents within this anthology or in case of any complaints, grievances, or objections, neither the anthology editor nor the publisher is to be held responsible.

Contents

Editor's Note

The theme of this book started as something I thought I'd always keep locked in my head, but as it is evident, I didn't. I never thought I'd actually compile and edit a book. Compilation seemed like something that would require a great deal of effort and time and I felt like I wouldn't be able to do justice if I took up such a project. Editing proved to be the most difficult part of this entire process. At one point, I even thought this won't work out. But it did. So here we are.

When I saw quite a lot of my friends compiling, editing, and writing their own books, the urge to see my name on the front cover of a book that could soothe people like me became irresistible. I already knew which publication I wanted to work with. The only issue then was the theme.

I had originally thought of compiling this book based upon a social issue, to be honest. The idea of putting out this theme into a book just popped all of a sudden. I somehow knew this was always there in my head, but I don't think I ever said it out loud. And now, thousands of people are going to be reading this and I can't wait.

The book 'Beneath the Layers of Me' is about self-love. About shedding the various layers you've guarded yourself with and not only discovering but also embracing the real person within.

Meet the Editor

Jumana Presswala changes her residence as per her new favourite fantasy novels. She's an aesthete, an avid reader, and a writer. She finds solace in words. Her desire to discover unusual words and preserve them in her writings is quite peculiar. She enjoys weaving and exploring fantasies. Besides reading and writing, she's also passionate about capturing nature and skies in her camera in an aesthetically pleasing way. You can always find her thoughts and unusual words on @fantasizingwriter on Instagram.

Poems

Medo

by Teresa Terly

The thought that one day my soul would conquest scares me
The thought that one day my rent would depart scares me
The thought that I am dubious about letting my guards down scares me
The thought that my kindred spirit would stop loving scares me
The thought that my love would edge off scares me
The thought that there would be no one when I fall back scares me
The thought that the ones who say, 'Close your eyes and I'll be there,' now turned into a jest scares me
The thought that I'll be eaten up in this role-playing scares me
The thought that I get worn out of humankind scares me
The thought that opening up and being termed as a prattle scares me

The thought that I get covetous scares me

That thought that I'm turning into a sham scares me

The thought that one day, my whole existence wouldn't matter...scares me.

Nevertheless,

The reality of having courage and being kind is more magical than unicorns and sparkles

And

The fact that you are so endearing raises the bar to make this world a better place to live in.

It's a step. Everyday.

Love Yourself

by Sarah Siamwala

Dear soul,

Learn to love yourself first,

Start respecting yourself,

Start appreciating yourself.

The more you respect yourself the more you can love yourself.

The more you get to know about yourself, the more time you give to start discovering new things in and around you.

Knowing your worth is important so that you don't compromise with things, rather you push yourself up and chase it.

Set boundaries and deny things you aren't comfortable with.

It's time to put yourself first.

Avoid negativity.

Let the bad times go off.

Focus on your goal.

Do whatever pleases you even if it doesn't make sense to others.

You will be designing your destiny.

So don't tolerate disrespect,

Not even from yourself.

Privileged Fame and Hard-Earned Victory

by Lakshmi Yazhini

The stars and the moon swept the desert sky,
At night, the Atacama was a party hall,
Where the stars and Selena frolicked,
Their lustrous attire glowing at one and all
Selena shone in her long white gown,
Leaving a trail of moonlight on Earth,
The stars couldn't help but glare at her,
A tad jealous of her noticeable girth.
Orion with those twinkling eyes said,
'Oh Selena, how bright you shine.'
Arcturus toasted, 'Your brilliance doth cover even your flaws,'
As he tipped his gleaming glass of champagne.
Proxima, winking at weary travellers sighed,
'With you next to us, our sheen doesn't seem enough.'
While Ursa Major's tears glistened as she cried,
'You're ubiquitous, but us others take the snuff.'
Selena's serene eyes eyed her fellow stars,
As she said, 'Oh this effulgence isn't mine,

This gown is but a reflection of Helios' work,
Who burns so hot, while I just reflect on his shine.
My dear stars, while my gleam and fame are borrowed,
Do remember, that your light is your own,
The moon may be everywhere, a commoner in the sky,
But a star is rare, because of wage, not a loan.'
The stars agreed, enlightened and proud,
Because the Moon is admired, but the star is searched for,
Combusting and burning, they made it to the sky,
Although, just a twinkle, glinting with candour.
Thus ended the dialogue, between the stars and the Moon,
Reminding us that hard work trumps privileged Fame,
While we might shine bright, it's just a reflection
Of all those before us, who etched their name,
But luminescence of our own requires work,
A process of toiling, slaving, and burning bright,
It is true, that not everyone notices our glint,
But those who do, always smile with delight.

From the Drop to the Deep

by Lakshmi Yazhini

She said goodbye to the Mama Cloud,
Whose swirling emotions made her bawl,
Making her escape from her mother's embrace,
To Humidity's delicious but filling haul.

Papa Wind showed her high mountains and vales,
Sister drops raced her beneath the skies,
But bigger she grew and heavier she became,
As she neared the Ocean's watchful eyes.

'Come to me,' it said, 'This is your end.' Consider
But she thought not, she wasn't ready to perish,
Many gardens to visit, many humans to caress,
Before she embraced the Ocean, expiring a splash.

Thus, is human life in a gist,
To a drop in the ocean, from a soulful mist.

Beneath the Layers of My Mind

by Anakha Raj

Beneath the layers of my mind
Nothing was within me other than sorrow
During this sad time, my inner voice started talking to me.

But beneath the layers of my mind
I started to recall my past
A life which was filled with negative emotions
And then it started to approach me now
The sequence increased minute by minute.

Beneath the layers of my mind
I need to keep myself positive
But loneliness hugged me so tight
Depression had eaten my mind
Happiness being washed away by tears.

Beneath the layers of my mind
There was so much pain which was deeply touched my heart
I smiled every day but was never happy
For me now, everything became impossible.

Beneath the layers of my mind
The voice just screamed and said,
'Break all the barriers of sorrow
Live the life as you dreamed
Fly high like a free bird.

Just take a deep breath
Throw away the thoughts of loneliness
Now let's start a new beginning
Evolve as a new human.'

Beneath the layers of my mind
Now the smile was back on my face
Joy was all around
And now started to live in my thoughts.

There is Always Another Way

by Srushti Chavan

Why must we wait for our luck to shine?
When only we can erase our crimes
A ladder of hope waits for us to climb,
It's always there even at the worst of times.

Why do we think of ending our story?
When we still have the rest of our lives to rise with glory
Why do we let our fears push us down?
When all we have to do is get back up and pick up our crown.

Whenever you feel you have lost your way,
Remember, there is always another day
Yes, time does keep going by
So, buckle up, and tie up your own tie.

Every day, remind yourself
Your life cannot be ruined because of anyone else
The people who scarred you aren't worth your tears,
So why let them become one of your fears?

Life is not an exam we need to pass
It's a game we chose to win
Your marks don't prove your class
Thinking different from others isn't a sin.

Why must we hide behind a mask?
We are doing it wrong, that's not the task
The challenge is to stay true to yourself
It speaks plenty more than any trophy sitting there on your shelf.

Don't live in fear and sadness
Instead, lead your life with faith and happiness
Whenever you feel you have lost your way,
Remember, there is always another day.

Behind the Curtains

by Fatema Setranjiwala

Sitting in the audience,
Wondering what's happening behind those red curtains.
A voice mumbled to my ears,
A few sayings someone offered me.
Unbarred the door of a closet found some toy cars worth ten pennies,
Lost a box of treasure beneath it.
Janitor's wife decided to cover his deeds for the rest of her life,
When her soul departed into broken pieces beyond
A letter in prison was found to be sorry for herself.
An open book also has hidden pages,
But only a close book is judged by its cover.
Not one but thousands of masks are worn,
Real or fake it is yet to decide.
And the curtains drifted their way giving the play a start,
But what arose backstage will always remain a secret.

Imprisoned

by Ben Holdeman

You said I would never be free
That I would never be
Anything more than what you see
The only problem with that decree
You never had the ability
To know the spirit inside of me
So, I walked away graciously
You didn't deserve anything more
Then surface simplicity.

Emotional Statue

by Michael Girasoli

Public persona
Iron, strong, unbreakable
No hurt penetrates.

Concrete foundation
Built to last the test of time
Strong mind and body.

Titanium will
Leader amongst followers
Your safety and light.

Sheltered from danger
Beacon of light in the storm
Casting fear away.

Is anyone here?
Are the layers visible?
Believing I'm alone…

Journey to the truth
Time to peel back the onion
Who's behind the mask?
A scared little boy
Trapped inside a mature man's
Body lost inside.

A layer not seen
Camouflaged by bravado
Witty humour helps.

Daily struggles hurt
Without them, there is no growth
Embrace life's beauty.

Be true to yourself
Behind the facade with love
Follow the music.

Loving the Self

by Spruha Rajwadkar

Witnessing the fleeting eyes towards her
Thinking of what and how she did up until this moment
She ultimately stood still and relaxed
Looking at her reflection in the huge
My gleaming eyes, the way her hair fell on my shoulders
A shiver went down her spine
Then and there, she froze.
Recognising the girl who stood ahead
Knowing it hadn't been easy to love herself
It was a journey she hopped on
With next to no glory left
She starved and she caved
As it became harder for her to be slaved
Among the norms that society created
What she cared about was all she represented
And that was it.
She wouldn't hesitate
Nor would she fixate on being perfect
She was herself and that was what she needed to be.

She Can

by Insiya Arsiwala

When she looked into the mirror,
What did she see?
She saw a girl,
Trapped inside herself, never free.

She grew up being her own worst critic,
Always looking down on herself,
For she was surrounded by talented people,
And she'd never felt so small before.

All she wanted was to be happy,
To feel loved and accepted again
But the world is cruel,
Leaving her alone, with nothing left to gain.

'It feels like I'm losing my passion,' she thought
'Losing my meaning
Once again
I've lost myself.'

At that moment,
In the stillness of the night,
She heard a soft voice say,
'The night is the darkest before the brightest morning.'

She looked back up at herself in the mirror,
Her eyes filled with a new-found resolve,
For she was strong,
And was determined to never give up,

She thought, 'Stop hating yourself for everything you aren't,
Start loving yourself for everything you already are.'

Whispering to herself, she uttered,
'Life is short,
Happiness, even shorter
So, why not start by accepting yourself?'

Muffled

by Anju Elizabeth Kurien

This is not an exaggeration, it's real.
You will sense it
Every cell
Of your body scream,
Nobody will understand you
The way you lose your loved ones.
In the most insensitive way,
Is the scariest,
You will lose it.
In the end, you may turn numb
You may feel you are going to die,
If you don't cry,
But you won't, you can't.
Emotions seem too strange.
There is no way till you vent out.
But it won't be a solution.
Rise or fall apart in the end,
Realise, it's a phase

You have to go through,
You alone, all alone
Fight those demons,
Sit back and relax,
You, a beautiful soul,
With everything you need
Inside you, search for it.
Stop blaming the powerless you
Hey, you are just tired
You need to swim
Never lose courage,
Though you might
Find yourself lost
You may look around and see
Nothing but that endless blue
Oh, dear! Don't give up.
Fight the demons,
Oh, beautiful soul!

So, What if I Am?

by Suhani Shah

Dear you,

So, what if I am?
A mirror built by the world's reflections,
So, what if I am?
A little more you than I'm me
Because
Today I fell in love with the universe around me,
I looked a girl in the eyes and as she laughed, I felt myself fall,
I saw a boy winking at his friend and I fell in love, just a little,
A friend told me she was having a bad day and I hugged her tight,
Someone waiting for you outside class or at a bus stand,
A silly joke or comment made just to make someone laugh,
I fell in love with the stars,
In the way, my mother told me to have a good day,
In the way, my teacher talked with such sincerity,
I fell for the sky,
And the person skipping down the road on the way back home,

For a toddler staring out the window in awe of the world around him,
For the stranger who waved at me in the hallway,
A barista's smile as he hands me my drink,
A bridesmaid's tears at her best friend's wedding,
So, what I am?
Everyone I see
So, what if I am?
A little more you than me
I fall for it all. I fall for me.

Love,
Me.

Confining in this body

by Giuseppe Li Santi

Confining in this body
Would be a limit,
Identifying with this body
Would bring suffering,
Despising this body
Would be offensive,
Idolising this body
Would be selfish,
Welcoming this body
As a channel
For perception,
Living in this body
Is the way
To transcend it,
Immersed in an ocean of intuition.

Light As Nothing

by Giuseppe Li Santi

How many things in me
Hidden by darkness,
Sunken treasures
Without maps to consult
With the conviction of a diviner
I go into the slopes
Following a word, a thought,
An intuition without a name
Reason guides,
Desire illuminates,
The mind follows
Up to the threshold
Beyond which it is necessary to
Undress
And become light
As nothing.

Feels Like Home

by Rana Dhvani

I feel I am stuck between love and practicality
In the twenty-second century, everyone strives for a personality

Whereas I just want a person to be my little dream
No logic, no lust, just like my home, so serene

But of course, that won't happen because here we are
All stuck and between distrust and devoid of faith we are

We dream of happiness, but we don't know the source
Our days worked up like a mess and our lifestyle is coarse

The inner parts of us just desire some freedom
But we won't let ourselves free for no reason

Just as we believe in barter and not in faith
With moto, if there's no advantage, it's not for my sake.

Relinquish Pain

by Rajshree Nipane

The journey of our love wasn't tough
Yet the efforts weren't enough.
Concealing my emotional mess
Feelings were noxiously wrecked.

Agony and despair keep me awake
I wish to escape this painful cage.
Pondering thoughts evokes anger
Those feeding my dark monster.

If you see right through the facade
Smiling with melancholy is hard.
Mind and heart are in warfare
Better not lose myself in despair.

Still, I stand up, to keep on giving
Even though I am left with nothing.
I don't blame my circumstances
Maybe, it's life's way of giving chances.

This City Is Not a City

by Erin Staley

This city is not a city.
It is many buildings built of Lego stacked one over another.
It is a collection of playing cards about to topple.
It is a mob of animated Sims with glowing halos who plot each other's deaths.
The murderer is your best friend.

That school is not a school.
It is a burial ground of 8 a.m. coffees and nervous breakdowns.
It is mounds of concrete moulded like playdoh over grated asphalt.
It is the smell of artificial plants shivering in the corner of a frigid library.
I think I smell my heart burning.

My home is not a home.
It is a labyrinth of dusty hallways painted with sugary smiles that melt and stick to the floor.
It is a culmination of false dreams and artificial hopes glued together with ruthless ambition.

It is a mother's miscarriage of idealistic parenthood.
And I am the child she lost.

A father is not a father.
He is a shrouded figure in the doorway holding the lightning bolt
he used to shake the sky.
He is the man with the iron glove that crushes your throat.
He is gorged on repressed emotion and watered-down love.
The air is cold where he walks.

My body is not a body.
It is a battlefield of fallen soldiers and scars that scorch the skin.
It is a lopsided image of a plastic doll I threw out at ten years old.
It is a tomb built over a film of grief.
No one mourns for me.

My Inner Self

by Shabnam Islam

'Silence'

Silence is what I hear,
Through the chaos and cheer.
They may not seem to talk,
But they speak a thousand tears.
The shore of memories down the lane,
Or the phantom of the world.
They are so many stories untold,
Yet the silence is caught in some fresh hold.
The screeching screams nor the pain,
Could break through the numbness of restraint.
It seems so peaceful and calm,
Where you can hear only your sound.

Aurora

by Shabnam Islam

'Aurora,' that's what she was called
A beaming light of dawn.
She knew her worth, yet she never knew herself,
Raging against the world and fighting for her quest.
Will she ever win, or the battle will go on?
A question arose inside her like an everlasting swan,
She removed her cast and rode the maroon colt,
She is ready for another battle which was on hold.

Invisible

by Shabnam Islam

Why can't I just vanish into the air,
Not seen or heard by anyone I care about,
I wish to be never seen nor to be heard,
Just be a memory from the past
And never to be stirred.
It won't pain, nor spark misery
Just be a leaf which will be blown
Away from the treachery.
Why can't I be just a mere pass
Which blows away with every timelapse.
It would be so easy for a kind like me
Never have to please anyone with its frozen empathy,
Be an unknown in this world
And seem like a droplet in the large.

The Girl You Don't Know Of

by Sakina Mahableshwarwala

Beneath the layers of me
There is a girl
Who just wants to be noticed by the world
Not a day goes by as she calls for me
I hear her saying 'Hey, let's show them something new today
But I get so shy so scared
The fear of rejection I'd say.

Beneath the layers of me
There is a girl
Who just wants to be free, someone who can openly dream.
She has asked me countless times 'Can I do this for myself?'
But I get so frustrated so tired
I shush her down, bury her deep inside.

Beneath the layers of me
There is a girl
Who just wants to be loved and accepted,
She keeps pleading with me to fly free
But the chains bound to her feet hold her back
She trashes around in hopes that I'd set her free
But I shut her out trying to remind her, who she is and why she can't do that.

Beneath the layers of me
There is a girl
Who wants to love who she wants to
Without being questioned about it
She wants to be free from the shackles of this world
She wants to confess her love loudly
But I quiet her down telling her that she would be judged for it.

Beneath the layers of me
There is a girl
She has dreams, she wants to travel
She has hopes, she wants herself to be marvelled
This girl, oh she is like a breath of fresh air
And she wants the world to know that
So, I tell her I'll eventually give her a chance
And soften her for now.

Beneath the layers of me
There is a girl
She wants to soar among the clouds
Be someone that sits with the stars, plays around with the moon
But I push her back telling her that they wouldn't want to do that with her
Making her see that she is not worth it.

Beneath the layers of me
There is a girl
She wants to run wild and live happily.
She wants to be herself and live freely
This girl, oh she is so amazing
She goes beyond you and me
So, I'll wait for the day to come when I finally let her open and set her free.

Inner Me

by Ayesha Anam Althaf

I love crying in the rain,
Because when I do no one can hear my pain.
You can see me smile,
But couldn't see the sadness inside.
Sadden as hell,
But for no one, it rings a bell.
I am not perfect,
I am not always correct.
But I am the best at what I do,
Even if it were for a few, I do.
I am proud of my heart,
It's been stabbed, hurt, and broken, but it always discards that and knows to make a new start.
If you could read my mind,
You would be in tears with what you would find.
There is always a pain that I feel,
But there is no one to help me to heal.

'The Her' in Me

by Krushita Sampath

In a pensive frame of mind, she cogitated
Recollecting the flakes of perception stacked upon her
Each piece weighing colossal pain
Pain drenched her skin
An amalgamation of a petrifying acumen they shoved into her bones
Still and all, I cherished her
With beautiful affliction gathering every thread with love
Love to darn the wrecked material, her existence
Her subtle eyes, fragile senses, and ceaseless courage
Radiated immensely as she rose to leave it all back
Love and adoration filled her heart, but for nobody
This time the love was for her,

For the first time, it was all about her
She looked more gorgeous than ever
Precisely flecked with the gems of tranquillity
Discernment knocked on the door of her heart
A heart that was woebegone, dejected
Was now filled with hope, to procure what she lost
Startled by her attributes, I fell for her
For 'the Her' in me
Yes, me.

The Invisible Veil

by Kriti Bhatia

Walking through the crowds,
Masking myself with an invisible veil,
Curtaining myself with the hues of artificiality.
My acne screams out loud, I shush them with the makeup patch.
My scars radiate a song of melancholy, I shut them up with a blush pink shade.
I look into the mirror,
She's a stranger, staring at me with her red-eyed rage,
A stranger who was once me.

They call her beautiful, they call her pretty,
Makes her drown in a plethora of anxiety,
For she knows, they praise the lies, they praise the hoax perfections,
For she knows, it's all a sham.

But her eyes hold misery as if wrapped in unending agony.
She holds back that teardrop, choking herself,
She calls out for love,
She pleads for affection.
For those bitter truths, that she kept hidden from the world.
For those imperfections, she kept within herself.
She crumbles her fist, out of frustration,
Her nails make a mark on her palm, signalling self-loath.
She screams silently, but it's loud, it echoes in her soft red cave.

Now, she walks into the crowd again,
Lifting this veil of "pretty lies",
Flaunting her flaws.
They pushed her to the ground,
Like a stoic,
She stood up back,
Breaking the chains she was tied in.

I look into the mirror again,
She smiles as if singing the melody of life,
Her eyes hold love now, love for herself, the real self.

Free, at Last

by Klaudine Palma

Quarter past midnight
And the minute hand struck
Right where it hurts most
The knot that keeps it all in check.

And then it untangles
Loose ends turn into tiny sharp pieces

Walls crumbled; mask fell off

Revealing the inner child
In the corner, holding her knees
Close to her chest
The safest she could ever get.

Quarter past midnight
She was set free
As she ventures out in the open
Free of walls, of inhibitions

The loose ends hit like bullets
Slowly, then all at once
Missed shots, bullseye
Unable to contain herself, she fell

Flashes of blinding lights
Exposing reality

Behind the walls, with her guard up
She was safe

Outside of it, bare and naked
She feels alive

After all, she is human
Made to feel and survive.

Dark Roads

by Fatima Mackizadeh

Coffees consumed
Cigarettes absorbed
Pills devoured
More, more, more
Bars all around
Escape not found
Mind a battleground
Run around, round and round,
Take the bridge from fear corner,
All the way to tear town,
Drive down dark roads,
Slumber comes not, toss, and turn
Burn, burn, burn,
Body alight, no respite
From this obsidian night.

Blues

by Fatima Mackizadeh

My mouth moves, moody
Words fall out, empty
Will I ever be happy?
No, not even close
Sugar, butter, salt, devoured
Professors and psychics, shamans (healers) and mosques,
Popping paracetamol, you confound us all
Yet the question burns a hole
Talk, talk, talk,
Blah, blah, blah
Eat this, do that, think this, feel that
I've tried it all
Fresh air, fresh air, you need fresh air
Get on the road, the wind will blow the blues away
I go and go and go and go
But no, no, no it's still all there.

Rejection

by Fatima Mackizadeh

I plunge in,
Risk assessed doom guessed
Bets are off
All or nothing, all or nothing
I take a swipe, wet beads wiped
Stomach fluttering, nausea impending
I look at my watch, tick tock
Bomb drops, my world rocks
I am facing rejection
Two flaming wings, my earrings
Turn me red, red
Eyes to the ground
Sweat and tears mingling
Earth eats me, sky sucks me
Water I beseech thee
Vanish me, vanish me.

Rage

by Fatima Mackizadeh

Slowly at first
I feel it pulsing in my veins
Exploding in the brain
Searing frenzy,
Coursing through me
Bellowing expletives,
Wind drowning my rage,
Hurling it back
Die, die, die,
Why, why, why,
Reliving the blame,
Reliving the shame,
Flinging the phone,
Punching the pane
Bone on bone,
Blood gushing in my mane
I destroy what remains
Venom spouting,
Softly cursing again and again.

Believe in Yourself

by Asad Umar

When this life becomes an arduous journey
All your plans get ruined adversely,
The rain of hardships has bedraggled you
And the world came trembling too.

The atramentous of pessimism has kept you on hold,
A catastrophe of the past has made you cold,
You are yet to make a story untold,
A tale of blissfulness by being strong and bold.

Onto the crepuscular roads, the dream lies,
From the amort of ashes, a Phoenix will rise,
Trigger your incentive and start taking action,
Struggle itself is the ultimate gratification.

Look for the possibilities rather than limitations
The real treasure lies beyond hesitations
You will achieve your feat; believe in yourself
Trophies of glory will shine on your shelf.

Me – Beneath the Layers

by Arwa Ratlamwala

Caught beneath a mortal
My soul wants to fly
No boundaries, relations
No fake or real emotions
Buried under social complications.

Someone untangle me
For my soul is tied with heavy pebbles
I try and try
To set myself free
I want to be just me.

Every day, I wander
To find my true self
But fail because I find myself
Through them.

The shell that was given to protect me
Soon became my identity
If I come out of it
I'll be a misfit
And the world won't like it.

The shell is hard and difficult to break
For the shell is made of dos and don'ts
That I have to undertake
I feel weak and demoralised
But it's not too late to realise.

Minds full of narrow lanes
That cannot even bare
A girl with an opinion
To justify their rejection
They use her appearance.

At first, I thought the layers are on me
But I noticed that the layers are
On their eyes
It solely belongs to me
How I want to see myself.

An Ode to My Distorted Self

by Khushi Kalra

Standing in front of myself,
I contemplated, 'No girl, you ain't yourself
What's up with this dieting and all?'
Friends in my head said,
So, he could take you to the ball.
Is he worth these calories burning?
What else would you do with your belly bulge?

The constant battle in my head
At 3 am in bed.
Sobbing to death,
On my pillow wet,
Why me? Why do I look like a bear?
Bears are cute, isn't that enough for me to care?

Bless your delusional heart,
The world, today, isn't for cute and smart,
Hotness is considered the only art.

Curves like an hourglass
High heels and makeup 'a lot'
Go girl, you look way too hot.
Boys going to go head over heels,
Seeing your skirt up those knees.

But remember,
Neither a pole nor a food hole,
Not too much of breasts,
Not too little of ass,
Oh, come on girl be a little sass.
Not too dark and not too light,
You ain't chocolate or vanilla delight.

So that people don't gossip,
Put a little more makeup,
Not too much.
Just enough to hide those pimples with a magic touch.

Don't forget to let your hair down,
For the guy from another town.
Just let it flow with your gown,
So that he entitles you with a crown.

A voice lost for years finally spoke up,
Whispering in my ears,
Darling! Don't waste your tears,
For so-called dears
'Your body needs to be perfect' it may appear
Do what your heart tells you.
Advice is given in every nutshell,
Bid their opinion farewell
And see your life flourish without their spell.

You may have forgotten
The freedom so long hidden
Flaunt your hair
Or be reserved in a bun.
Whatever outfits you want you may wear.
Be you. Be yourself.

Everybody is unique,
Have no more worries about physique.
So next time you catch yourself looking into the mirror,
Put all the thoughts in the blender,
Because you already have an answer,
That you are still pretty, whether thicker or thinner.

My Journey

by Misbah Iram

Spent my childhood being a perfectionist,
Which took over my real identity.
Packed my aspirations in a school bag,
Setting aside fun, joy and hobbies,
Focusing on math and science.
Although today, as a teenager,
Being much aware of my existence,
I am exploring myself.
Realising, I forgot to look at myself clearly,
Those scars and imperfections,
Were also a part of me,
They belonged with me.
Regretting, I had questioned myself earlier,
What are the inner desires?
Piled up in the corner of my heart.

Being apathetic about unwanted opinions,
Has been quite challenging,
But never a major issue,
How I advise myself matters more.
Learning to accept everything about myself truly,
Cognizant of what I feel like,
Veracious about who I am,
I feel alive for the very first time.
Not guilty of unknowing my recognition,
I begin this journey of self-love.

Our Layers and Unmasking Ourselves

by Komal Joshi and Rishika Priyadarsi

As children, we are the most inquisitive and the most unfiltered we could ever be,
With no barriers in mind, so far we could see!
Back then we had no worries in the world, no responsibilities,
In our life as we saw endless possibilities!
As time went on,
We sadly had to grow up,
Breaking the dream of the most perfect fairyland!
Remember when nap time was the only highlight of our school day?
No signs of worries at bay!
Studies, exams, jobs, careers, the world opened up beyond our rooms and comfortable bed,
Plus, a hell load of other drama and pressure was added on instead,
Slowly we were forced to alter and fake,
And some days even mask our true selves just,
'What was all this for?' you ask

To fit in, make friends, make our loved ones happy and live our "perfect, happy-go-lucky life"

Our old unfiltered soul and mind are now a hideaway,

And the perfect getaway,

Where we shut, hide, and confide,

In a total alter ego personality building up a façade.

The façade—the arcade of books, loud music, binging on movies,

Hanging out all day and night with friends, doing crazy all-nighters, partying and clubbing 24/7.

One or the other, or for some, all of the above is now our thing,

Or should I say our only escape!

Drug addict, being a full-on alcoholic,

Becoming a complete and carefree rebel without a cause

And whatever else that creates that illusion of a "happy world"

Some may go to that extent in hopes

That they can drown away all their burdens on their shoulders.

Everything else that makes us frown

And turn our world upside down.

Beyond those short never lasting chaos causing moments,
Once all that fog that's in our minds is gone,
We have that ray of sunshine and clarity
Just after that awful hangover, of course
That's how we sadly find and understand,
Who truly is there for us to keep and cherish,
And let go of all those fake friends and false ones,
At last, there some days exist,
The only option, you know what I mean?
So, hold up before it's too late and before you,
Yes, you do or say something that causes pain and chaos,
And unimaginable regrets to anyone,
And most importantly, yourself,
Take a long deep breath,
Think of all the good things in your life
Those that truly love and care for you,
Count your blessings not your problems
Remember you're an amazing human being,
Not a pressure cooker or some uncared leftover
Say goodbye to all this crap
But now is the perfect time to maybe start over?

So, before our life flashes before us once and for all,
That too before our time is truly up,
Say what's pent up in your heart,
Just go for it and stamp, act upon it
Before it becomes a good old mix up
Get up, wash up, dress up,
Pick up from where you left it,
Before all this chaos started
Do whatever is your "pick-me-up"
Don't be too harsh on yourself!
So, what if your grades aren't of flying colours?
So, what if you don't have that Mercedes?

Or that CEO post and that fancy house?
Or that "picture-perfect life" or that "fairy-tale ending"?
It is your life, and you need to create if perfectly

Let's peel these so-called layers,
Like the way, you peel whilst chopping and cooking with onions,
Yes, you'll cry,
Yes, you might hurt yourself at first,
But you are just like you are when you put your mind, heart, and soul into
Something,
Yes, the layers can be tricky yet messy to deal with,
But remember that God won't give you anything you can't handle.
Unmask and de amour yourself.

Who Am I?

by Ananya Singh

Beneath these layers, I'm searching for myself.
Yet, every piece I find is lost forgotten and broken
I'm longing for these feelings which have been suppressed in a layer of grief.
I have lost my mind searching for my missing piece.
With every flower that blossomed, my heart sank deeper until I couldn't look back
Misery awaited me while I hung on a thin string of hope
I hoped my scars would heal but a lifetime has passed by, and my soul is wounded.
Let me see the world from your eyes, I had forgotten what it looked like.
I showed you all my layers, yet I still wonder, 'Who am I?'

Back Story

by Riya Dugar

Everyone has a story
The one they don't share
The one that influences their decisions
And designs their character
As though it's not a story
But a true architect, a sculptor
Carving the mind and shaping the heart.

This story hides deep within,
Guarded behind a lock and key
But yet it wants to be found,
Playing hide and seek,
Waiting for that sun which will shine its light upon it
And discover the treasure
But you see, there is no map for this hunt
Instead, you stumble upon it,
Recklessly but cautious enough.
Carelessly yet careful enough.

You open that box
Knowing what you'd find
Still so surprised by the revelation.

The question is what do you do with this story?
If it becomes your treasure or
A meaningless box
Added to your memory collection.
Remembered now but forgotten with the ageing time.
Will you guard it with the same tenderness as the person who hid it?
Or will you sell it away as something expensive yet not priceless?
Will you let this story be your architect and your sculptor?
Or will you itself become the one who shall carve a new treasure and hide it in his heart?
Deep, engraved, playing hide and seek somewhere waiting for it to be discovered.

The Secrets We Hide

by Arfa Fathima A

The deepest of our emotions,
Speak to us when we are alone.
We know not what exactly they want,
We know not what exactly we want.
Because the only way out of this conflict,
Is to let them out.
But do we really want to?

I know of those times,
When I was heartbroken,
When I was trying to heal my broken soul.
But it never did happen,
And never will.

Situations take control of you,
They don't let you live in peace or joy.
But what will you do,
When you have to let them out,
Oh! boy,
Because the only way out of this conflict,
Is to let them out,
Let out the secrets we hide,
The ones we surely can't abide by.
You know of those guilts you've felt,
You know of those tortures with which you've dealt.
Then why let them kill your inner peace,
And let yourself get into another inner conflict.

It's not just you out there,
Fighting those dreadful battles every day.
Maybe someday you'll regret it,
For not letting them out.
And just fighting them,
And letting them kill you from inside.
And to prove that to you,
I could keep a thousand bucks bet.

Don't let yourself dry,
Like autumn trees and dead bodies.
By letting them ruin you,
You'll just make yourself unworthy copies.

It's never too late,
For not always letting it up to your fate.
Because the only way out of this conflict,
Is to let them out,
Let out the secrets we hide,
The ones we surely can't abide by.

Stories

Finding You

by Siddhi Patil

It's seven in the morning. And this is yet another beautiful day in Kaira's life. She wakes up, looks at the mirror in her room, gives a little smile, and then to the kitchen to make her favourite morning tea. She stands there still waiting for her tea to boil staring at the beautiful morning sky. She strains the tea into a cup and starts walking to her balcony where she finds Nemo, her dog and her only best friend. She always receives a warm welcome from him. As she goes further to sit on her bean bag, she starts sipping her tea. Nemo sits on her lap comfortably.

Kaira starts petting him and sighs, 'It's another day, Nemo.'

It feels as if he understands what she has to say despite doing nothing but licking her hand. And when she looks at the clock, she notices that it's already 8:00 a.m. She hurries to get ready for work. And just like every other day, she says goodbye to Nemo before leaving.

It seems like a very normal day at work. Everything is as normal as it could be, everyone is busy with their work; the office is in a hurry and just like every other day, Kaira goes to her desk without anyone noticing her. As she starts working in her prettiest cubicle, her boss arrives and announces that they got their new client and it's finally time to celebrate, inviting them to a party at the nearest bar. The environment in her office all of a sudden becomes cheerful. But just like every other time, no one notices Kaira, nor do they bother to ask her. She continues working and a few hours later, she heads to the coffee machine where she finds a colleague, Shreya. There's an awkward silence, and her colleague finally breaks it.

'So, are you planning to go out with them?'

'No.'

'Are you free to go out tonight?'

'Umm, actually I got some work tonight. But we'll see each other later sometime.'

There's another awkward pause before both of them just grab their cups of coffee and leave.

The same evening, she reaches home, gets comfortable, pours herself a glass of wine, and sits there with Nemo. Time passes, and there's still the same pin drop silence since she reached home. Nemo breaks the silence with a little bark and tears start rolling down her cheeks and she starts sobbing. Nemo, without making any noise just goes and sits on her lap. She hugs him and starts crying again. Now finally she's able to talk.

'Why am I like this? Why can't I socialise no matter how hard I try? Why do I have no one except you who can understand me? No colleagues, no friends, no family, it's just me and you. And that makes me so uncool that no one likes me or notices me. I just hate living like this!' After listening to her Nemo does nothing but try to comfort her with his presence. She pours herself another glass of wine and sleeps there itself.

The next morning, she wakes up with Nemo on her lap and sun

rays beaming over her eyes. She looks at her phone and realises that it's a Sunday. Today, she calls Shreya to have lunch with her. She is so anxious since this is the first time, she's doing something like this. She realises she's reset the pillows on her couch ten times in the last twenty minutes. And finally, the doorbell rings and Shreya arrives. Kaira welcomes and asks her to make herself comfortable. Shreya sits there on the couch and Kaira rushes to bring her some water. She comes with a shining glass of water. She shivers as she gives that glass to Shreya. And as Kaira had imagined earlier, she spills the glass of water on Shreya's clothes and her favourite couch. She starts panicking and can't stop apologising.

All of a sudden, Shreya blurts, 'Stop! It's completely alright!' There's an awkward silence before she asks (rather demands) Kaira to sit down and close her eyes. 'Breathe. It's completely fine. There's nothing to be worried about. It was just a glass of water. Calm down. Breathe in… and now breathe out. You're fine. And now slowly open your eyes.'

When Kaira does, everything seems much better. Shreya offers the same remaining glass of water to Kaira. She accepts it and thanks Shreya, responding with a kind smile. Nemo arrives and starts jumping on Shreya to greet her and she falls back on the couch so that Kaira has to pick Nemo up. Shreya seems to be shocked, terrified, and speechless.

Kaira begins to shout at Nemo, 'That's not good Nemo! You better apologise!' Nemo makes a sad noise and starts licking Shreya's toes. All of a sudden, they start laughing. Finally, both of them sit on the couch. There's an awkward silence between them for a few minutes.

Shreya breaks the silence by saying, 'You never told me you had a dog.'

'It's not just a dog, he's my best friend.'

There's again an awkward silence. This time Kaira breaks it by complimenting Shreya's dress.

Shreya smiles, 'Looks like none of us is good at small talks.'

Kaira gives a small smile.

All of a sudden, Shreya cries in excitement. 'You like books!'

Kaira is standing there shocked as Shreya runs towards her bookshelf and starts looking at her books.

'You've got a nice taste.'

Kaira just starts looking strangely at Shreya and asks, 'You like books, too?'

'Yeah, I love them.'

Kaira asks, 'What's your genre?'

'Fiction and thriller. What about you?'

Kaira replies, 'Well, you can see it now; we have a similar taste.'

After that, the two spend hours talking about books and checking out almost every book from Kaira's shelf. When they look at the clock it's already 5 in the evening. Kaira asks Shreya if she would like to eat something. That's when Shreya realises she's hungry. They spend another twenty minutes arguing about what to order and still can't come to a decision.

In the end, they settle for Maggi Kaira's comfort food. Kaira makes Maggi and coffee for the two of them. Shreya plays with Nemo while Kaira cooks. Kaira comes back within fifteen minutes and all three of them just sit on her balcony and enjoy the sunset with their food. No one speaks for a while.

Kaira suddenly blurts out, 'Thank you so much, both of you.' Shreya gives her a questioning look. Kaira emphasises, 'No, seriously, I wouldn't have thought I can have a good day with a person and now, at least I have one more person who could be my person and make me look cool'

Shreya says, 'You were always cool with me and without me, you are always going to be cool. You don't need to prove to others that you are cool it's never about how others see you but it's about how you see yourself and how cool you think you are. And as long as you think that you are cool, then no one else matters. By the way, this Maggi is amazing.'

They sit together for some time. Shreya leaves after a while.

The next day, Kaira wakes up, smiles at the mirror widely, makes her morning tea and goes to Nemo to wish him good morning but today she says, 'Today is amazing. Let's seize it!'

Don't Be A Mirror

by Harshit Dudhani

'He had a great life. Abhi, I see him in you, he taught you a lot.' A 50-year-old man said to me, staring into my eyes earnestly, taking my hands in his and caressing my thumbs. My eyes were filled with water, but I nodded and gave him a hint of a smile. I passed along all the guests, trying not to catch their eyes, so full of pity for a fatherless child. There were so many promises made to my mother and grandmother of being in touch, so many reassurances of being there for us were given and sympathetic, pitiful looks were exchanged every time they thought I was looking the other way. I was standing beside my mother helping her stand as she was sitting completely numb while eyes filled with water, leaning against the wall.

'Papa! See this large T.V. It must be so much fun to binge-watch cartoons. I need this same piece.' A kid, maybe of 7, said to his dad. Everything seemed to fade into the air as I was recollecting the time when I used to ask for every cool thing that I saw from Dad so that I could show it to my friends. My dad was not a millionaire or something, but he used to earn well, now I am on my own. I realised how time changes, and no one can stop it. I remember asking Dad for a G-Shock watch worth rupees. 7499 as few of my friends had already purchased it. It was the December of my 10th grade.

Dad had said, '*Chhote* (kid),' he used to call me with love, 'You have boards in 3 months, and you are tempted for a watch. You should focus on your studies, and I will get it for you if you score well.'

'But... all my friends have it.'

'So what? You already have a watch, and you should wear it. But... I guess you need to show it off, right? People don't even earn this much money in a year and instead of cheering and praising for what you have, you are demanding more and more. If you can't fit in the group, you should leave it but stop being fake, *Chhote*. It will destroy your reality.'

'Sorry to say this, Dad, but if you can't get a watch for me, it's fine but no need to cover it,' I said with a heavy heart.

He gave a hint of a smile and said, 'Okay, if you score above 85%, I will get you the watch. It's a deal.'

Later, he came into the room with a plate filled with food as I skipped my dinner. 'May I ask you why you skipped your meal? Have you started dieting?' he jokes.

I reply, 'I won't eat until you get me the watch and I won't even study.'

'It's your loss, buddy, not mine, and I know what you told your mom; I was not expecting this nonsense from you. Go and take your watch from the dining table.'

I was about to stand and run towards the table when he intervened and said to finish the dinner first. I ignored him and ran towards the table. After wearing the watch on my wrist, he said that this is the last time he was tolerating this nonsense behaviour. I was happy about the watch and was imagining my friends' reaction to seeing it. I was unable to sleep at night because of excitement.

Similarly, I got an iPhone 6S and other gadgets as well as expensive clothes. But from today, I had to fulfil my dreams and take the family's responsibilities on my shoulders. After 12 days of mourning, I was about to go to the office. As everything was going to be new, Mom gave me *Dahi Chini* (curd mixed with sugar). It's an ancient practice for whenever you start something new, basically for a good start.

The office manager updated me with everything about what happened in the last 12 days. There were 3 meetings scheduled for the day, and though I was broken by heart and was not in a condition to meet anyone, I made myself realise that if I don't give my best, we may have to pack our bags and leave this city. At the end of the day, I was drained out and meetings were not up to my expectations.

Days passed by; my responsibilities increased along with the load of work, and yet I was learning how to handle the office and manage this company. The good news, i.e., slowly, and steadily, I was learning everything and was about to ace the skill. A year was about to pass after Dad's demise and the business was back on track. It was Monday, 11th June 2019, and a meeting was scheduled with the director of ACU LTD. I also had a personal question for him. The office was situated on the 19th floor. The director of the company is the same person who said Dad taught me well. The meeting went well, and I showed the courage to ask the question.

'Is this stability of mine what you saw in me or it's something else? Because you told me that you see my dad in me.'

'Oh! Don't worry, yesterday you made me realise that I was wrong.'

'Yesterday? We didn't even meet yesterday, what happened yesterday?'

'Try to recollect, Mr Abhishek, after parking your car in front of The Royals Café, when you were entering the café with your friends, there was a beggar who asked for your help but when security was resisting him and trying to throw him out, you stopped them and gave the beggar a note.'

'Yes, a note of Rs. 500,' I interrupted with joy.

'That's appreciating. But the problem is that you slapped another poor child who was asking for help when you were going back alone after paying the bill. Is it because you were surrounded by people for the first time, and you wanted to look like a charitable person with a golden heart and you slapped a child the second time because you were alone, and you thought no one was there to judge you?' he asked in a disheartened tone.

'No, Uncle , the child grabbed me by my right leg and my trousers got dirt marks. He was irritating me.'

'So, you slapped a child who was maybe hungry all day just for asking you a favour? And if I am right, you were wearing these same trousers and I don't see any mark on them.' I was sweating after noticing his observation skills.

'But how do you know all this?' I asked out of curiosity.

'I was with a client, sitting at the window seat. I was wrong about you, Abhi, but now I know who you are.'

'So, what was I supposed to do?' I asked, brokenheartedly.

'Abhi, a child like you who had always been eating with a golden spoon will be like this, you just care about your image, maybe you just want attention and people should think that you are a great human, and they will accept the fake you and will consider it as real.'

'Sorry to disappoint you, Uncle,' I said after taking a deep inhale.

'I am also sorry for being so harsh, come on, let's go for a walk.'

A BMW X3 was waiting at the doorstep of the office building, but surprisingly we didn't take it. We took a right and were walking towards the complex gate. We kept walking for about 900 m to 1 km and what I saw was a completely different world. It showed the real difference between rich and poor people. They were bottom of the poverty line; it was a remote and transferable setup. The old men were lying on a plastic mattress placed on the footpath while children were half-naked and playing with each other; laughing and enjoying, and women were sitting in a group and chitchatting, waiting for their husbands to bring food for their family.

'Abhi, have you noticed that they all are happy with their lives though they have a lot of problems? They enjoy every moment; they don't wait for something great to happen to be happy.' He told me that he comes to this place every week and I was shocked because this place stinks like hell, garbage littered all over. Later, we went to a cemetery where a boy was performing the last rituals, probably of his father, this scene was very emotional as it reminds me of my father as I performed his last rituals a year ago.

'Abhi, what do you see?' I was numb and was not able to speak, I was just looking at the young boy who was not more than 17 years old, he was shouting and screaming, and tears were flowing continuously from his eyes and liquid flowing from his nose, he was begging to God for his father's life. A 17-year-old helpless child whose grandfather was old enough to feed the family.

My eyes pooled with tears on seeing the young boy.

'Abhishek.'

Mr Chopra was calling me. 'The man is leaving the world of greed and illusion, is there something he is carrying with him? The man maybe was trying to impress, like you are trying, but can you see any one of those near him now? Some old people are probably his uncles, a few children who are his nephews, a few other people who are maybe his close friends or other relatives, but none from those whom he was trying to impress, and no one standing there would have left his side after knowing his financial status because they are his loved ones, and they are always supportive no matter what. Abhi, try to be authentic in a world that celebrates superficiality so that you are true to yourself in every moment, and you will be able to share your deepest and truest part with others. I know a man is a social animal and we all love being surrounded by people but don't try to fit in where you do not belong just because of peer pressure or family pressure in a situation where you are compromising yourself. Take a stand for yourself, believe in it, and fight for it, if you are alone, it's fine but you are being yourself and fighting for yourself because if you can't stand for something, you will fall for everything. Even Alexander the great said, "When you bury my body, don't build any momentum and keep my hands outside so that the world knows that the person who won the whole world had nothing in his hands while dying."'

All these words blew my mind as I realised, I was not living my life and was just trying to impress others around me, I was not being myself as I was trying to be someone else's reflection—like a mirror. I didn't have any goal or aim to achieve, just tried to be someone's destination, I lost myself by trying to fit in somewhere I don't belong. I degraded myself for just being surrounded by people. Appreciation became more significant to me rather than improvisation. Most of us make the same mistake, but we should understand that by improvising we will upgrade ourselves and we will be more useful to others and people will appreciate our help and work. We must try to not run behind appreciation, run behind excellence, and then appreciation will come to us. Everything and everyone will fade away one day, it will be just me for myself, so I must work on myself and be an asset to humanity rather than trying to be someone. Create my existence.

Show Me What I Am

by Aanika Gajendragad

Her head throbbed as she heard laughs around her. 'Do our homework for us, or else,' Saanvi warned. She fell to the ground as her enemy kicked her stomach and walked away.

'You better give it by the lunch break,' Rekha said in a sing-song voice, kicking her left shoulder. She felt the world go blurry as her eyes shut.

'Why are you late, Amaira?' her math teacher asked when she entered the classroom.

'S-sorry sir, I had a stomach-ache,' she stuttered.

'Lies. All lies. Stand near the board.' Amaira sighed and nodded. This was the fifth time in the week she got scolded for something she didn't do. She looked at Saanvi and Rekha, who tried to hold their laughter. 'What are you doing?' her teacher asked when she wasn't coming to the spot. He asked her to.

'Oh, Amy, I am sorry for the trouble I caused you,' Saanvi whispered mockingly when she neared them. She threw her bag on her table which was in front of Saanvi's and Rekha's, unfortunately, in frustration and cringed at the nickname. 'Behave, Amaira. Stand outside the class.' Her teacher ordered. At this point, she felt like crying. She could do nothing but listen to the snickers of the people she hated the most.

'Your principal called. He said you were rude to your chemistry teacher. This is the second time this week, Amaira,' Her mother said when she came back from school. Amaira groaned, plopping on the couch. 'You were such a good child, what happened to you? We pay the fees for you to misbehave?'

'Mom, leave me alone. Please.'

'Am–' She let out a loud shout, interrupting her mother. She ran up the stairs and into her room, shutting the door with force. Leaving her mother in shock. She immediately burst into tears.

'Why does everyone treat me like that? Am I that bad?' she spoke to herself, looking at the full-length mirror in front of her bed. 'I guess it's because I'm fat.' She held her waist. 'And ugly,' she added, wiping the tears from her cheeks. She thought she saw the reflection in the mirror blink when she was well aware she wasn't blinking. But she shrugged the thought and threw herself on the bed, kicking her legs in irritation. She eventually fell asleep.

Rubbing her puffy eyes, she found the time to be 7:30 p.m. 'Start doing your math homework.' She ignored the voice in her head. 'I said, do your math homework.'

'There's no use, I'm not going to school ever.' She fought back to her mind.

'Don't be ridiculous. Go, do it.' Regardless, Amaira took out her phone. Within seconds she put it back down and proceeded to walk to her table. 'What am I doing? I'm not going to attend school.' She thought to herself.

'You were being stubborn. I had to take control,' the mind said as if it had a voice of its own. She started doing her homework, and to her surprise, she knew every sum. But that couldn't be possible because she hated math. And she was awful at it.

'Amaira,' her mother called out, knocking lightly on her door. 'Come for dinner, sweetheart. I'm sorry for shouting at you.'

Amaira's red face soon turned to a soft one as she replied, 'Yes Mom , coming.' Her mother let out a gasp in shock.

'What the heck is wrong with me?' Amaira asked herself, hitting her head multiple times. 'Hitting it won't do anything. You'll only harm your head.'

'Who are you? Get out! I don't want to eat!' She shouted to her head. Anyone near her would think she's a psychopath. She waited for her brain to respond as it did before but to no avail. 'Are you alive?' She asked it. There was no response. 'Thank God.' She slept on the bed with a sigh.

'Amaira! Come on, the food will get cold!' her mother said.

'I'm sick of my name being used so much now,' Amaira mumbled and shut her eyes, not caring to respond to her mother. She looked at her legs as they got out of bed and started walking towards the door. 'What? Stop, stop walking. Don't move,' she scolded her legs, hitting them to make them stop. The legs didn't listen and continued to walk as if they had a mind of their own. They walked until she forced them down. She only fell on the stairs with a loud thud, causing her mother to look up in alarm.

'Ugh, you're so stiff-necked.'

'So, you're not dead,' she said out loud.

'Who's not dead?' her mother questioned. Amaira shook her head and climbed down like nothing happened when she was burning from embarrassment inside.

'You're doing something good for once.' The voice in her brain observed as she picked the piece of bottle gourd from the plate. Just hearing the voice made her change her decision. She immediately put the piece down, to which the voice spoke, 'You are such a birdbrain.'

She scoffed and answered, this time making sure she didn't say it aloud, 'Look who's talking about brains.'

'Shut up, I'm not your brain. I'm just inside it.'

'Who are you, a ghost who invades people's brains? Get out of my brain.' She thought to herself. She felt stupid arguing with her brain, or at least someone in her brain as the voice claimed.

'I'm you. Just better. I'm perfect.'

'I'm you. Just better. I'm perfect.' She mimicked the voice. She found her hand reaching for the glass of water which soon splashed on her face.

'What was that for?' She asked the voice but got no reply.

'You okay, honey?' Her mother looked concerned.

'Yeah, I am. I'm fine,' she breathed. She just nodded and went to wash the dishes. Amaira went back to her room.

'It's time you show yourself, ghost in my brain,' she said once she closed the door to her room. She didn't get a reply. 'Hello? You don't speak when I ask you to.'

'Go to the mirror,' she heard the voice say.

She did as she was told. She knew it wasn't her reflection in the mirror. She was a lot slimmer, and a lot prettier too. The voice wasn't lying when it had said it was perfect. The reflection truly was. That explained the blinking of her reflection earlier. 'Who are you?' Amaira whispered, touching the mirror with her soft hands. 'I told you, I'm a better version of you,' the reflection replied. The mirror didn't act like one. It was like it had been turned into a window. The reflection was moving around while Amaira simply stood there. Suddenly she felt a sharp throb in her head, the world went white for a second. Then it was back to normal again. 'I'm back.' Her brain said.

'Get out! I don't want a mirror reflection inside my mind.'

'Aren't you tired of being the one everyone always scolds? Aren't you? Don't you want to be known as the perfect one? Why does it have to be Saanvi or Rekha?' the voice spoke. Now that she thought about it, Amaira did want a normal life where everyone treated her well. She nodded unconsciously.

'Good. Then let me take over you. Let me control you and make everyone like you.'

'Okay.' Amaira watched as her legs took her to bed. She instantly fell asleep.

She woke up with a splitting headache. 'Amaira, you're up yet? You have school today, remember?' her mother shouted from outside the room.

'Mom, I don't want to go. I will wake up, Mom,' she said. Her mother was surprised, and so was she. Until she remembered she had someone living in her brain.

She got out of bed with a light head, dreading going to school. But her ego took over. She wanted to become the best.

'Bye Mom , I'm leaving!' She said, holding a slice of bread in her mouth.

She walked to school with a clear mind, knowing that her perfect self will correct her.

And it did. She improved in drawing (which she was bad at, just like any other subject), and sports and she also argued back with Saanvi and Rekha. Which she would never have done. Her classmates started to accept her as one of their own, they even included her in the Truth or Dare game they always played. But Saanvi and Rekha hated this new form of hers. Perhaps they were jealous. They tried to harm her more. (Keyword: tried. Amaira only held them back with the strength she had.)

This continued for two weeks, and everyone seemed to be fond of her.

Amaira sat at her study table—her body in her room, her mind someplace else. 'You are being stubborn again. One minute I stop controlling you and you're already somewhere else.'

'You just love the word stubborn, don't you?' she asked her brain.

'I love it when I'm the one calling you stubborn. Forget that. I think it's finally time for you to control yourself. I've stayed long enough now and trust me, your nerves stink.'

'You can smell my nerves? That's disgusting,' she hissed.

'Not the point. I mean half the point but not the point,' the voice said.

'Well, then what's the point?'

'I want you to be you. Not me.'

'You do realise we're technically the same, right?'

'We aren't. I'm the better version.' Amaira groaned at that.

'Yeah, yeah, Miss Perfect.' She rolled her eyes.

'It's time for me to leave your mind.' The voice insisted.

'But people are so nice to me. They will hate me if I turn back to normal again. I can't lose you. It's like saying Superman lost his ability to fight.'

'So, you used me? I was just a way to get people to like you?' The voice angered.

'Wasn't that why you invaded my brain in the first place?'

'I wanted a friend, Amaira. Believe me, this might sound stupid, but being locked up in a mirror is not fun. You know what, forget it. I'll be in your mind for as long as you want. You're my "master" after all.' She was enraged. Amaira didn't speak as guilt took over her.

Amaira knew she didn't feel like herself. She knew she wasn't the one gaining the courage to do everything. 'Hey,' she whispered to her head when she was in the washroom at school the next day.

'Miss Perfect, you there?' She tapped her head. The voice in her head hummed in response.

'As much of an arrogant little witch you are, I'm thankful to you. You made me realise that with just a little courage I could completely change what people, except for those two brats.' At this point, she didn't care about the looks people shot her as they passed by her talking to herself. 'I don't think I need you anymore. I'm sorry for yesterday, I shouldn't have used you like that. I'll be good from now and I'll make sure you don't get in my brain again. Feel free to talk to me from the mirrors.'

'Aww, but it's hardly been a month. I enjoyed controlling you.'

Amaira chuckled. 'I question your mood changes. Come out,' she said.

Her head throbbed once more until she opened her eyes and looked at the mirror in front of her. 'Thank you again.'

The mirror self-waved at her. 'Go,' Amaira said impatiently when the mirror self wouldn't stop waving.

'Geez, okay! But seriously, I'm proud of you. Until next time, then!' The reflection replied and disappeared, leaving Amaira to look at her imperfect self. 'I like me,' she declared. 'No, I love myself.' She walked out of the washroom with pride. No one even noticed the difference in her attitude. She was her perfect self.

Celeste

by Remnik Gill

This girl. I remember when she was younger and used to come by the park and sit by the large maple tree. Her father would read to her. It brought her joy, sitting on the soft grass and listening to her father's smooth voice telling her glorious tales about beautiful princesses and wicked queens.

'Ellie. Your father and I are separating.'

At 10, she stopped coming to the park. And wasn't quite sure why. It's still the same thing if she reads in her room instead, she told herself. It's still the same even if she's reading alone now.

'Celly, we are moving to an apartment. You can still call your father, but you won't be able to see him.'

At 13, she stopped reading. She got busy, she told herself. Her friends didn't like reading.

'Here, Cece, come to my costume party!'

She went to their house dressed as an elephant. It wasn't a costume party. They pointed at her and laughed while she brushed her tears away. She ran back home and rushed to her room.

'Where are my books, Mom?'

'I threw them away, Lettie. You spend too much time in your room.'

She cried herself to sleep, mourning the girl she was before this she let the world hurt her.

At 15, she began wearing makeup. She enjoys makeup, she told herself. It'd been a year since anyone saw her bare face.

'Hey, Elle. Will you be my girlfriend?'

'Yes.'

At 17, she began applying to universities.

1. Your unique passions or interests.

2. Strengths and accomplishments that you can illustrate with stories.

3. Unique details that capture your personality and help you stand out.

She didn't quite know what to write in her application essay. Could she ask others for their advice? No one knew her. She was sure they didn't even know her name.

Her name was Celeste.

She couldn't blame them, she thought. She didn't know herself either.

Her name was Celeste.

Who called her that anymore?

Her name is Celeste.

The Main Character

by Fatima Mackizadeh

I decided to go see him on impulse, my boyfriend of three years. Taking a deep sigh, I logged off my computer, turned around to see Anita, a colleague of mine who lived in the same lane close to his house, about 60 kilometres away in Hubsville. I asked her, 'May I take the train with you? I am going to see my guy.'

Anita was a big girl, tall and imposing, with chocolate brown skin, and a dark mass of curls tied in a tight ponytail. She pursed her lips, and nodded, 'Yes, of course, come.'

She went on staring at me, thick eyelashes framing her brown beady eyes. I felt her study my face like she was trying to read my thoughts. Or perhaps I was overthinking, as usual, I smiled, 'Thanks.'

Seeing myself in the mirror, the white harsh lights not helping, dark circles more pronounced, my lips seemed thinner than I remembered. I brushed some lipstick on, patting the rest on my cheeks trying to bring some life back to them. I had at least lost 10 pounds in the last few months, the dismal array of cold food offered at work not having helped, though sometimes I would give in and eat; overeat, even.

We left taking a shorter route and got the train right on time. I took it as a good omen. I felt grown-up. This was the first time I was doing something like this. People did it in movies, just showing up unannounced. The train flew, a mechanical horse with wings, the windows, and doors of the carriage wide open. It was still dark, and I shivered, pushing the hair off my face.

Anita asked, 'Did you call him? Is he coming to get you at the station?'

'No, not yet.'

'It's okay. I'll drop you. He lives in my lane, doesn't he? I have seen him a few times at the grocer.

'Yeah.'

'So, he lives by himself?'

I nodded, 'Yes.'

'Do you know anyone else in the area?'

'No, not really.'

I was getting antsy with all the prying and stared at my phone. 05:19 a.m. It was always past 19 minutes when I looked at the watch. Always.

She gave up, my monosyllabic responses helping, and started talking about herself, how she always lived in Hubsville, with her mother. Relieved, I zoned out. What would I say to him? Would he be happy to see me? Or just irritated as he was always nowadays, ignoring most of my calls, barely replying to my text messages, rarely making plans for the weekend, saying he was tired, or had a stomach-ache or the latest, or needed to spend time with his parents. My line of questioning usually ended with him calling me crazy, saying it's all good, and that was that.

After my goodbyes to Anita, I walked. It was a good 5-minute walk from the gate to the apartment building where he lived. I climbed the stairs, standing outside the door. It was so quiet that I could hear the TV. A sitcom was playing with the recorded laughter starting and stopping after every sentence the actors said. Just then, I heard him chuckle. He was awake. I knocked on the door, expecting him to open it, but I heard the TV go silent, and that's when I knocked again. No answer, and then again. I tried calling him, hearing his phone ring through the door and him not answering it. My heart was pounding, my stomach in knots. Why wasn't he answering?

Finally, he opened the door, blocking the door and not letting me enter, two cups of vanilla ice cream with Hershey's chocolate sauce sat melting on the coffee table behind him. 'What are you doing here? It's not safe to travel alone so far at this time of the morning.'

I saw red. After six months of frustration, loneliness, and gas lighting, suddenly it was clear. He was cheating on me. There was someone else in the apartment with him. I spotted a yellow-coloured plastic mosquito bat, the kind imported from China. Ducking past him, I entered the room and picked it up. I brought it down on his arm and didn't stop until it snapped into two. I threw it down and somehow, the thick magnified convex glass on my watch had cracked. He just stood looking at me, cowering. He was scared. I could see that. 'Anita knows, doesn't she? She has seen you around with her,' I yelled.

He mumbled, 'I didn't want to hurt you, I thought you might try to commit suicide if you got to know, but I love Tara…'

I turned and ran. I had so many questions. My ears flaming with rejection and shame. I was older than him by a couple of years, maybe that's why. I was not pretty enough. My usual list of insecurities running in my mind. Three years of unconditional love and all I had been left with was heartache and betrayal.

Why, why, why? I asked myself again, hoping my brain which was always quick to give me insight, would answer, but there was silence, tears flowed mingling with my lipstick, and I could taste salt and caramel-flavoured beeswax. I dashed past the gate to the highway, skidding on my black heels, I stopped. There was a mild rustle of wind, the sun was coming up, the road was deserted, and a dragonfly flitted by.

I looked at my watch it was 06:20 a.m. I knew just then that I was going to be alright.

Acknowledgements

Kudos to myself for doing this despite everything I'd been going through at the time when I took up this project. Huge thanks to everyone who supported me during this process including my parents, other members of my family and all my hype friends. I am so glad to have discovered amazing friends and writers during this process. Grateful to the co-authors for deeming this book worthy of their amazing pieces. And of course, the Inkfeathers team without whom this wouldn't have been possible.

Meet the Co-authors

Michael Girasoli

Michael first embraced his love of words when he was in his twenties. He always loved reading but never really fancied himself a writer. In January 2020, he decided to finally put the pen to paper. A whole new world opened up for him. His first book "Girasole-A Walk Through the Seasons" was published in December 2021.

Kriti Bhatia

She is Kriti Bhatia, a 16-year-old. A student of life, she started writing at the age of 13 as a way of escaping reality and pouring her thoughts down in her diary, and there was no stopping since then. She also loves to explore and try out new things that make her happy.

Giuseppe Li Santi

Giuseppe started writing when he was a teenager as an act of emotional survival. Music was also an important aspect that accompanied him during his life to become an explorer to achieve a process of knowledge and learning in himself, on that line where form and essence meet and where energy and matter blend.

Klaudine Palma

Klaudine is fond of reading fiction and poetry as it gives her different views on the world and takes her on a lot of adventures. Eventually, she engages in writing, mainly to express and relate, until it becomes an outlet to discover personal answers to complex human emotions and experiences.

Suhani Shah

Suhani is a young girl from Mumbai, India. She is often found lost in her imagination or listening to music and sketching portraits which come to life in her writings. She hopes people find just as much comfort in reading her words as she finds solace in writing them.

Krushita Sampath

Krushita has been in love with books and poems since she can remember. She's a person who loves to write on topics such as love and fantasy. Books and poems for her are "the place" where she finds comfort. Writing about romance and self-love is her flair. Fictional characters always tend to intrigue her. She says they teach her not only about love but also about how love is given and how life is supposed to be lived. She fancies penning down her feelings in the form of words.

Harshit Dudhani

Harshit Dudhani is a learner as well as a writer. He hopes that everyone finds happiness in little moments of life and should stay away from worldly things as this is being happy for real. He believes that from cradle to death life is a struggle and this struggle is known as life, so enjoy it and live every moment and cherish memories.

Remnik Gill

Remnik is an aspiring author. When she's not writing, she can be found at a local cafe, reading a romance novel, or running around a bookstore, obsessively telling her friend the plot of every book she sees there. You can chat with Rem on Instagram at @journalswithrain.

Anakha Raj

Anakha Raj is a 22-year-old girl currently pursuing her BDS degree. She is an ambitious and passionate girl who loves to write poems and express her feelings through poems. The ultimate aim in her life is to publish a book.

Misbah Iram

A 14-year-old empathic and inquisitive teenager, Misbah is from Bangalore and is currently in ninth grade. Passionate about writing, speaking, psychology and volunteering, she enjoys participating in events and meeting like-minded people. She truly believes speaking and loving herself has helped a lot to embrace her identity.

Anju Elizabeth Kurien

Anju Elizabeth Kurien is a PG scholar and an admirer of art who seeks self-expression through her drawings and words. The world of pencils, pens and blank papers is her asylum. Most of her writings accompany her drawings posted on social media platforms.

Teresa P. Terly

Teresa P. Terly is a student and also on her way to being a jill of all trades by adding a writing feather to her hat. She pursued her degree in English Literature, Communication and Journalism and currently doing an MBA. An energy bomb and keeping her heart on her sleeves with a pure soul. Getting inspired by her friend was the best thing that finally got her to bring her pieces out to the world. She hopes that you all enjoy the writing which would motivate her to sketch down more.

Lakshmi Yazhini

Lakshmi Yazhini is an avid reader of genres like fantasy, science fiction, mystery, and contemporary literature. She deeply appreciates the works of poets like Emily Dickinson, Robert Frost, William Shakespeare, William Wordsworth, and many others. She likes to dabble in writing, reading, dancing, and reviewing in her free time. Yazhini is currently a student at IIT Madras and is pursuing an MA Integrated Program in the Humanities and Social Sciences department.

Aanika Gajendragad

Aanika is a 14-year-old aspiring writer. She's home-schooling at the moment to focus more on her career as a writer. She has written many short stories and a few novels now and also has a story published in an anthology. She has a website where she writes blogs, muchbyaanika.com.

Asad Chaugule

Asad is an Automotive Digital designer by profession, along with an interest in sketching cars, Asad has a flair for writing poems in English/Urdu and goes by the pen name of Assad Omar. Asad loves exploring nature to enhance his creative skills in designing and writing.

Ananya Singh

5 years ago, Ananya Singh decided to inspire and comfort people through their poetry. They found great joy in reading and writing. They aspire to be a great author one day. Ananya Singh is a Vashi-based poet who has been writing stories and poems for four years. Their work has appeared in several anthologies, and they have begun posting poetry on Instagram at @_subliminal_lines.

Srushti Chavan

She is an inspired writer who feels immense pleasure in writing about emotions, nature, and the motives of people. She makes sure that all her writings are encouraging and leave the reader in a happy state. She is an admirer of the art of music and literature. The main hobbies that define her are writing lyrics, stories, poems and singing.

Sarah Siamwala

Writing for her was just like breathing fresh air, an expression, and a survival essential. Through her words, she spoke volumes that occupied your mind and seeped deep into your soul. Thoughts you could resonate with, words that made you wonder and sentences that left a mark on your heart!

Insiya Arsiwala

Insiya Arsiwala is a young student in Mumbai, India. She has a passion for music, is an avid reader and loves writing short fun-filled and realistic stories and poems. Her main goal is to provide her readers with something that they could relate to or have experienced at least once in their life. She hopes that her writing can comfort them.

Ben Holdeman

Ben began writing a few years ago as a way to add a little creativity to his life. What began as a random hobby quickly became a daily source of inspiration and joy. This will be the second time Ben has had any of his work in print. Ben is from Ohio, USA.

Dhvani Rana

She would call herself a seeker—a seeker of knowledge, seeker of the truth, seeker of the source of those infinite, perplexing emotions one experiences every moment as one sails through. She is a person who yearns to know the way this totality works and is doing everything to understand it.

Erin Staley

Erin Staley is a Canadian writer, currently studying Creative Writing at Concordia University in Montreal. You can find her previous work in the anthology Pie in the Sky and on Instagram @empoetryy_.

Ayesha Anam Althaf

Ayesha Anam Althaf is a 17-year-old, science student from Bangalore. A self-made writer. Who loves writing poetry. A published poetess. A person who admires a good story. She enjoys listening to music in any mood and at any hour of the day. A fun-loving, kind, and caring person who enjoys spending time with friends and family but prefers to be alone so she may write and listen to music to express her emotions and sentiments. Ayesha loves to read books. She started writing poems and publishing them in anthologies. She plans to keep doing so in the future. She's also a Wattpad author whose work has been published. You can connect with Ayesha via:

Instagram: @anaalfa.writes

Email: anaalfa.writes@gmail.com

Wattpad: @anaalfawrites

Siddhi Patil

Siddhi is a student, writer, and entrepreneur. Writing this story gave her a different kind of joy because this story was more about accepting yourself the way you want to be and not about how others expect you to be. She hopes you enjoy reading this story as much as she enjoyed writing it.

Shabnam Islam

A woman with a pen of pain and pleasure with the ink of love and endless treasure, writing her way in the blank pages of her life, bleeding all up with her thoughts of twilight. Read it out loud or read it slowly, you will find something common with me in your life uphold. An amateur writer who is still on the venture of her life.

Fatima Mackizadeh

Fatima is a budding poetess born and raised in Mumbai. She started her career as a librarian and is a true bibliophile. She feeds her addiction by buying more than she can read. When she is not writing, she spends her time playing with her cat, Cake, and drinking coffee.

Arwa Ratlamwala

Arwa Ratlamwala is a homemaker and is blessed to be a mother of two beautiful daughters. She loves writing and tries to convert her feelings into words. She keeps her language simple so that it reaches and touches as many hearts and emotions of the people reading her. "Keep it Simple" has always been her motto. She tries to live life to the fullest.

Khushi Kalra

Khushi Kalra grew up and currently resides in the capital city of Delhi. Amidst all the hustle, she usually finds herself alone with her thoughts and doesn't hesitate to pen them down. She is that person who would work the extra mile to complete what she has sought to do.

Sakina Mahableshwarwala

Sakina Mahableshwarwala is a 17-year-old who likes to read and write during her free time. She uses abstract feelings and mood boards to help herself with the flow of her words. All in all, she hopes to make her readers attached to her words and make them feel as if she is speaking for them.

Rajshree Nipane

She is Rajshree Nipane from Raipur, India and is an interior designer by profession. She describes herself as a lifelong learner, an ardent reader, and also a budding writer. A coffeeholic entitled by @coffeemyalchemy on Instagram, her quotes and poetries are mostly metaphorical, blending with raw emotions, subtle reality, and subtle imagination all together on paper.

Rishika Priyadarsi

Rishika is a humanities student and a poet who started writing down her thoughts during the lockdown, given the amount of free time it provided! She loves writing and has written over 75 poems, some of which are published in various anthologies. Apart from writing, she finds solace in music.

Riya Dugar

Riya Dugar is a simple girl from Mumbai. She is a student, currently pursuing her master's degree. She believes that for the magic to work, we need spells. Words. So, writing is her way of bringing some magic into this world. She hopes her readers can find comfort in her writings.

Spruha Rajwadkar

Spruha Rajwadkar is a teen student who loves to write. She can always be found with a book in her hand or food sometimes even a cup of coffee. She is learning new things every day and becoming a better version of herself alongside. Surrounded by gazillions of opinions views and voices struggling to find her own yet growing and improving as she unravels new chapters of life.

Arfa Fathima A

Arfa has never been so fond of anything but writing. Writing has always been a form of expression for her. Being a person who always adored the art of writing, which arose from the keen writer's deep interest, she began to pen down her thoughts and imaginations. Everything she visualises and writes comes from her little dramatic world. Arfa is a strong lover of fiction and writing gave life to her own little world of fictional scenarios.

Komal Joshi

She is a creative soul with a spark of magic and the desire of doing more leaving a little bit of glitter smile and laughter wherever she goes. Forever a new girl on the block who loves Bollywood and all things media and who is always ready to lend a hand and try her 100% with a smile. *Gujju Chokri* from the UK but *Dil se* forevermore a proud Indian.

Fatema Setranjiwala

With a suitcase of thoughts, she decides to embark on her journey through words you'll love. Someone who loves creativity and adventure. Not so sporty but tries her best to run this race that is known as "Life".